ADVENTURES OF ROOP

The SEVEN MONKEYS OF SHERA

DR. HARMEET KAUR BHALLA

Published in 2022
Becomeshakspeare.com

One Point Six Technologies Pvt Ltd
119-123, 1st floor, Building No. J2, Wadala East,
Wadala Truck Terminal,
Mumbai, Maharashtra- 400037, India
T: +91 8080226699

Wordit Art Fund helps deserving authors publish their work by providing monetary support. To apply for funding, please visit us at www. BecomeShakespeare.com

ISBN - 978-93-5667-172-0

Contents

Chapter One

It was the month of December, and the winter vacations had begun. Roop's school was closed for two months. She was excited to live with her maternal grandmother during her vacation. Her grandmother lived alone on the outskirts of the city of Darjeeling.

Her Nani Mrs Seth was not quite old. She had silver-grey hair and a few wrinkles. She wore a white sari and golden spectacles.

On hearing the knock at the door one cold winter evening, Mrs Seth slowly opened the wooden door. Roop hugged her Nani tightly as she welcomed her, "How are you, Roop?"

Her mother carried her school bag and a small suitcase.

Roop screamed, "Nani…my Nani, I love you."

Mrs Seth held her hand and carried her inside. She made them sit on the two chairs placed in the living room. She went to the kitchen and brought a box of homemade sweets.

Roop quickly opened the box, picked up two, and said, "You have made my favourite sweets Nani."

They went to the bedroom, and Roop's mother placed her luggage in the cupboard. Roop started running all around the house. She was happy that she would have a good time with her Nani.

She went and opened the window. Mrs Seth knew what Roop was looking for.

Roop started peeping out and asked, clapping her hands, "Nani, I cannot see Monkey Uncle Shera. Where is he? How are Sunday, Monday, Tuesday, Wednesday, Thursday, Friday and Saturday?"

Her grandmother spoke teary-eyed, "Roop, I forgot to tell you that Monkey Uncle died last week of cancer."

Roop held her mothers hand and said, "How did this happen? This is very sad…then what about the monkeys…. Ramu is so young and not friendly with the monkeys…poor monkeys."

Her mother said, "Roop, he was sick…Ramu and his mother are there to take care of them."

"So many monkeys…they must be missing their master," said Roop in a severe tone.

Her mother gave her further instructions, "Don't worry. They will learn to live without their master. You will stay here for fifteen days. Don't go out alone and take care of your Nani."

"Okay, Mama.... I am big enough now," said Roop standing on her toes.

Her mother smiled gently and said, "No, you are not that big.... you have to study every day for three to four hours. If you have any problem, you can call from the landline number."

After an hour, they had dinner. Mrs Seth had prepared Roop's favourite vegetable pulao and Chocolate custard.

"Oh Nani, you cook so well," said Roop enjoying the delicious food. She changed her clothes, and as it was getting late, her mother wanted to return before the streets became deserted. It was already getting cold, and the temperature was dropping.

She kissed her forehead and waved her,

"Goodbye.... see you Roop.... take care."

Chapter Two

In the neighbourhood, Ramu lived in a small hut near the railway line in Darjeeling with his mother Sheela and father, Shera. He was twelve years old.

His one-room house had an attached small kitchen and washroom. Every day many trains crossed the railway line.

Since birth, he had seen his parents and their seven monkeys in his house. He went to a local government school as his mother wanted him to study.

His father, Shera, was a juggler and a famous monkey trainer. He earned his living by showing monkey dance. He was a favourite of children in several localities. He was known for his humble and generous nature. He had seven monkeys. He named them after the seven days of the week. He took them two at a time.

They were his only source of income. He loved his team of seven monkeys. He was considered to be a perfect human being. He never left his monkeys, even

if they grew old. His two monkeys Sunday and Monday were old now. They could no more dance, so they stayed at home.

One day he fell pretty sick; he called Ramu and said, "My son, I want you to take care of these monkeys…… don't sell them or leave them in the jungle…I worship them as they are my bread and butter."

After a few days, when he was in grade seven, his father died of blood cancer. All the monkeys sat near the dead body of their master. Ramu noticed tears in their eyes.

Ramu had never ever looked after these monkeys as he was always studying. He wanted to study hard and work in an office.

After the cremation, he came back home and hugged his mother tightly. He cried as he was unknown to these innocent creatures.

While still sobbing, he looked at these faultless souls and said, "What will I do now? I don't even know how to handle them."

His mother, too, started crying as her mind was overburdened with the mere thought of bringing up those who were left behind.

"We will work hard and manage somehow, Ramu," said his mother.

The following day Ramu looked up for money in his father's trunk, but he found only a few coins. He went out and bought bananas.

The monkeys were hungry, and he gave two bananas to each. He and his mother, too, ate bananas.

Ramu spoke with tears in his eyes, "Ma, we have no money. I think I will go to the zoo or sell them to other jugglers so that we too have money."

They both sat down and started admiring these seven monkeys. The monkeys began chattering on hearing the knock at the door.

"Open the door, my child…see who has come at this time in the morning."

Ramu found Roop and his grandmother standing as he opened the wooden gate. She was holding a packet of peanuts and bread.

Mrs Seth embraced Ramu and said, "Ramu, I hope you are fine. Don't worry…. I am always there to help you."

She looked at Sunday and Monday and said, "See them they have lived for fifteen years with your father. They are old and need your assistance."

Sheela came and caught the somewhat heavy packet from Roop's hand, "This is so kind of you, my child."

Roop walked towards the monkeys with Ramu. The youngest one Saturday sat on his shoulder.

Ramu started peeling the banana for him and said, "Roop see, I am left alone with them…. you can come and play with them till you are here."

Roop was excited to see them, and she pulled her Nani's saree, "Nani, we can come every day with some peanuts and bananas see how they love it. I can spend my pocket money on them."

Sheela pulled Roop's cheeks gently, "That is so kind of you…you are a beautiful girl with a kind heart."

"Yes, we can come every day. Let us go now," saying this, Mrs Seth held her hand and left their house.

Chapter Three

A week passed with Ramu being extra careful towards the monkeys as he could make out from their faces that they were sad after the death of their master.

Since the day Shera died, the other jugglers looked on these monkeys. Every day one or the other turned up to buy these trained and intelligent monkeys.

One morning he came up to his mother and said, "Mummy, I think I cannot keep these monkeys anymore. When I grow up, I want to do some other job. I will continue with my studies. I cannot earn my living by becoming a juggler. I will sell these monkeys."

"No, my son," shouted Sheela. "No…. I can understand the problems you face, but God will help us. I cannot live without them. It is your dads most precious gift for us. I will go out, earn money and fill their stomach."

After listening to his mother's statement, he made an angry face.

It was a bright sunny morning, and Roop was sitting with her granny on the terrace. She was doing her holiday homework.

Sheela, too, had tied the monkeys outside to the pine tree in the neighbourhood. She made them sit in the sun as the weather was pretty cold.

After every few minutes, Roop came to the boundary wall of the terrace and called out, "Monday.... Tuesday....   Wednesday......Thursday......Friday.... Saturday......Sunday."

All the monkeys looked up to her one by one. They hopped on hearing their names.

She clapped her hands and said, "See, Nani, they know their names so well."

She was jumping with excitement when suddenly she saw an old van stopping in front of their house. Two strangers got down and started calling out the monkeys by their names.

The first one was short, plump with black dyed hair and huge eyes. He wore black clothes, torn jacket and a muffler around his neck. The taller one was six feet tall with a rough coat, and he wore a long beige overcoat. Both of them were shabbily dressed.

Roop felt uneasy on seeing them. She quickly asked Mrs Seth, "Nani can I go and play with these monkeys. I have to give them bananas too."

"Yes, go, my child but come soon," said Mrs Seth.

Roop quickly picked up her books and ran downstairs. She opened the door and stood outside her house to look at the two men.

She stood behind a tree trunk. Then she tried to overhear their conversation as the short one said, "Danny, I think there is nobody around.... such trained monkeys.... they are perfect for our circus."

They pulled out a plastic bag from the van and moved towards the monkeys. They tiptoed towards them, and Danny said, "Sammy be careful.... Yes, better be ready.... I will bring them one by one.... we will quickly drive to our destination. Keep checking that nobody is watching us."

Roop saw ORIENT CIRCUS written in bold black letters on the van. She thought of the circus that was in the town at present. She had seen the posters of ORIENT CIRCUS pasted on the walls everywhere.

Roop loved these seven monkeys, and she could not see them in trouble. She moved a bit closer, but suddenly someone threw a handful of mud on her.

Then one of them said, "You are watching us.... now you won't see anything...you little naughty fellow."

Roop rubbed her eyes and shouted, "Help! Help! My eyes are hurting...Aunty.... Ramu...Nani.... come...I can't see anything."

She couldn't see anything as her eyes turned red and were full of tears. She understood that nobody had heard her voice.

She lay on the floor watching the two. The taller one came close to the monkeys and took out a perfume bottle from his pocket. He sprayed it on them, and one by one, all of them fainted.

As Roop could not see clearly, she felt helpless. She was unable to move from her place.

The two thieves pulled the monkeys one by one and dumped them in their van.

Roop kept lying in the mud and crying, but nobody listened to her. In the meantime, she could hear the sound of the van's engine. They had taken all the monkeys, and Roop lay powerless.

Chapter Four

On hearing strange sounds, Sheela rushed to see Roop howling. She caught hold of her and screamed, looking all around, "Roop, my darling, get up."

"Where are my darling monkeys? Where are they? Who has taken them? Tell me, Roop…. tell me." Sheela said, dusting off the mud from her clothes.

Roop was crying and trying to tell her neighbour about the loss.

She said, sobbing, "Aunty, those two have taken all your monkeys, poor animals, and I am sorry I could do nothing."

Sheela sat with her hands placed on her forehead on the ground and started crying.

She wanted to know about the thieves. She asked Roop, "How did they look? What will I tell Ramu? My dead husband must be cursing me."

Ramu came dangling his hands and feet but suddenly took a halt on seeing his mother crying with Roop.

"Where are my weekdays? Why are you upset?" said he.

Roop kept rubbing her eyes and explained the entire incident in detail.

"Do you have any clue, Roop?" asked Ramu giving a horrified expression.

"Yes, I saw Orient Circus written on their van."

Tears ran down Ramu's eyes when he said, "Then it is quite clear but still we are not sure. What will I do now? God is punishing me because I was thinking of selling them. They were my lifeline…. a precious gift from my father…. I have no source of income left…. maybe we die of hunger now, ma."

"Don't cry, brother….I have seen the two of them…. .I recognize them. I can certainly help you out. We can take the risk by going and searching for them in the circus."

Ramu spoke with his hands trembling, "Please help me, Roop…it is two o'clock…we can go to see the evening show of the circus."

Mrs Seth was unknown to everything but came walking fast as she heard Roop crying.

She embraced her and said, "Roop, my baby. What happened all of a sudden? How did you fall? Look at your clothes…your eyes have turned red."

Roop had turned quite normal now. She narrated the incident to her Nani. Mrs Seth was shocked to hear about such a theft.

"We should inform the police, Sheela. They have taken all seven. How could they?" she said.

Ramu came up to her and said, "If we call the police, we may waste time. Roop has read the name on their van. We have a first-hand idea that they belonged to the circus. Can we go to the circus? Please maybe I will find them there."

Roop wanted to take Nani's permission. Mrs Seth was a bold lady.

She said, "All of us will go."

Roop had never been to a circus. The evening show was at five o'clock.

They had three hours to go. Mrs Seth took Ramu and Sheela to her house. She made them sit and gave them chapati and dal to eat. They ate food with great difficulty as Ramu was continuously sobbing.

By four o'clock, they left for the circus in a local bus.

Chapter Five

All of them reached in half an hour. There was less excitement and more curiosity to have a look at his darling monkeys.

The Orient Circus was spread in a vast area. There was a lot of hustle-bustle with colourful tents and posters of animals all around.

In one corner, there was the ticket stall. Men, women, and children were standing in a queue. The place was quite noisy as vendors selling popcorn, ice cream, and balloons were shouting on top of their voices.

"Ramu, we have to buy the ticket first; we have to go inside. Maybe we catch hold of the thieves," said Mrs Seth.

She took out her purse and handed him the money. Ramu and Roop went to buy the tickets as they heard the announcement that the circus was about to start.

The loudspeaker went on, "Ten minutes…. ten more minutes …come and see Cheetah walking on fire…Ten Lions…horses…. a new attraction is waiting…. come… few more tickets left."

The new attraction made them look at each other. They kept peeping inside the tents to have a look. They soon thought of a plan.

After buying the tickets, they moved towards the entrance gate. The entrance was relatively narrow, and they could enter one by one.

They got seats in the first row. Mrs Seth and Sheela settled with the two children in the middle.

Ramu whispered something in Roop's ear, and she got up.

Mrs Seth asked her inquisitively, "Where are you going?"

She caught hold of her hand and said, "Nani, I am hungry. I want to buy something to eat. Please give me some money."

"Don't get lost…don't worry as we will surely take action once we see the monkeys."

"Okay," saying this, Roop went out with Ramu.

While coming inside, they had noticed an opening in the tent. Roop and Ramu removed the tent slowly and entered. They could see girls dressing up for their

ORIENT
CIRCUS

performance. They were giggling and applying make-up.

They hid behind a row of trunks so that nobody could see.

They knew nothing about the place. They had to reach the site where the animals were kept. They slowly moved behind the trunks.

Suddenly one girl shouted, "Who's there? Come out."

Ramu and Roop ran fast, and the girls ran behind them, but they quickly entered the spectator's section. They stopped following them as they went to sit with their guardians.

"Where are the chips and popcorn?" asked Mrs Seth.

"Oh, there were too many people buying, so we came back," said Ramu making a sad face.

The circus began with the orchestra playing loud music.

The first announcement was made, "Hello, this is the biggest circus in the world with five hundred animals. Enjoy the full circus. You will now see the great elephant Star with two small elephants, Tara and Sohni."

The music played, and a beautifully decorated giant elephant entered with two small ones. Ten to twelve boys entered dancing in pink dresses. They were carrying rings and footballs.

Ramu suddenly got up from his seat and said to his mom, "Mummy, I will go alone and buy the popcorn and chips…. Roop, you keep sitting."

Roop gave a sad expression. She wanted to participate equally in the search.

Ramu moved towards the entrance door with his one hand holding the ticket. He kept it securely because he would need it to enter again.

Chapter Six

Ramu looked all around to see if nobody was watching him. He wanted to reach the backyard where all the animals were kept. It was getting dark. As he slowly crept towards the vast area, he felt nausea. The place smelled of dung and rotten food. He covered his mouth and nose with his muffler.

He noticed four horses tied in one corner. He started walking by placing his feet carefully on the damp ground. In between, his slippers got stuck, so he had to pull them out. There were several cages with birds, rabbits, cats and dogs. He felt sad to see so many animals living strenuous lives.

Ramu's eyes were searching for his weekdays, his seven monkeys. They were nowhere to be seen. He stood outside the cage of the Australian parrots and started admiring them.

He soon became upset and lost hope as the monkeys were nowhere to be seen.

Ramu was walking carefully, hiding behind the cages and hay, but someone suddenly struck him on the back. Ramu fell on the swampy land.

"Ah Ah…please don't beat me…I am not a thief," said Ramu wiping his shirt and pants.

Two men caught him from both sides, picked him up and said, "You tiny thief…. how dare you enter our restricted area. You have come to steal our expensive animals. Get out, or we will call the police."

"Leave me, please…I just wanted to see these animals…. because I love animals…. please…. I will leave"

"Go, or we will throw you in one of the cages," said an old fellow with a long beard.

Ramu felt depressed and started crying. They brought him out to the entrance gate and shouted, "You better leave."

"Okay, Sir," said Ramu breathing heavily. He pretended as if he was leaving. He slowly walked towards the gate. He looked back to confirm that no one was watching him.

Ramu took out his ticket and entered again. His face looked tired. His mother was worried and caught hold of his hand and made him sit down forcefully.

His clothes were muddy, and she almost shouted, "Look at your clothes. Where are you going again and again? Sit down and wait for your monkey's turn. If we don't see them, then we will search for them."

Roop could make out from Ramu's gloomy expressions that he was unsuccessful in his mission.

One by one, the performers came and entertained the spectators. The tigers, lions entered with their trainers. They jumped across the ring of fire. It would have been a pleasure to watch if Ramu was not heavy-hearted.

As the following program was announced, the three clowns entered the arena. The children had a good laugh, but Ramu looked worried. He was bothered whether his monkeys had eaten something or not.

Roop couldn't control her laughter. The clowns began the magic show.

One clown came and stood near Roop and started dancing. She had a strange feeling about him. She remembered the short kidnapper. Roop stared at him and almost looked into his eyes.

She looked at Ramu and pointed towards the clown.

"He is one of them," she said, rotating her eyes.

Ramu was about to stand up when she ordered him to sit down.

The clown waved at the children gathered around him, then pointed towards Roop and said, "Hello doll…. come I will perform magic on you."

Roop felt uneasy, but she agreed when she saw one more girl of her age going into the arena. Mrs Seth, too, was happy.

The clowns made the two girls stand in the middle. They brought two massive trunks of brass. They were continuously saying,

Abra ka dabra

Abra ka dabra

The magic has begun

These two girls will now run.

The three clowns arranged the trunks in the middle. They opened the vast boxes and said, "Now see the magic…. the trunks are empty."

They started turning the trunks upside down to show that they were empty. One of them whom Roop was almost recognizing said, almost laughing,

"Come on…. you two brave girls…. jump in the trunk…. jump."

Some children clapped while others held their parents tightly as the girls jumped in the trunk.

The clowns made them stand for two minutes and said,

"Abra Ka Dabra

Abra Ka Dabra

The magic has begun

The two girls will now have fun

They made the girls sit down and close the trunks. They danced all around and continued to make people laugh with their mischief's. Mrs Seth, Sheela and Ramu stood up as they thought maybe they had taken a significant risk.

After three minutes, the trunks were opened. Many colourful balloons rose in the air, and people started shouting, "Where are the girls."

"Wait…. wait…. wait," shouted the three clowns." Sit down…. the magic is not yet over…hold your breath."

Chapter Seven

Roop and the other girl found themselves in a dark room. They thought they were in the trunk.

The other girl spread her hands and called out, "Please take us out…. the magic is over now."

She started howling, but on hearing her, Roop answered, "Don't cry. I think we are no more in the trunk…we are in a room. Give me your hand."

The other girl stretched her hand and caught hold of Roop's hand in complete darkness. She held her hand and started walking.

Suddenly the door opened with a bang, and one of the clowns entered holding a candle. Both the girls were startled.

He came close to Roop and said roughly, "You are the same girl…I know…we are not returning those monkeys."

Roop was familiar with the face, but she pretended to remember nothing. He was the shorter one who had thrown her down.

"Who are you? I don't know you," said Roop making gestures with her two hands. She had the confirmation that the monkeys were with them.

The clown felt relieved and caught hold of their hands. They crossed several rooms, and soon, they entered the arena.

The audience started clapping on seeing the two of them. The children shouted and screamed on seeing them.

"Ye…ye…they are back….they are not in the trunk."

The clowns showed the empty trunks to the other puzzled girl while Roop waved her hands. She was happy that they were almost successful in their mission.

Mrs Seth was waiting for Roop eagerly. Roop rushed towards her and hugged her tightly.

"Where were you, Roop? For ten minutes, we thought about what kind of magic this was.

Roop went to sit near Ramu and smiled at him.

Ramu anxiously asked, "Did you notice anything regarding my monkeys?"

She nodded her head. She said, "Ramu, you won't believe what happened inside."

Ramu almost stood up from his seat with his eyes wide open.

"What happened?"

Roop stood up and whispered something in his ear, and he smiled. She signalled him to sit down and said, "Let us wait for the circus to be over."

Roop answered in a positive tone, "It is confirmed that they are here, but we may have to inform the police in case if we fail to get there."

Finally, the last program was announced. The four of them held their breath as this was the last chance left to see the monkeys.

The announcement was made, "Hello beautiful men, women and children…. hold your breath now…. an outstanding performance of fresh animals from the jungle."

Chapter Eight

The curtains were drawn, and six people dragged two huge cages. The cages were covered with coloured cloths. The three clowns entered and started pulling the fabric.

In one cell were the seven monkeys, while in the other were four Pomeranian dogs. All the animals looked dull and morone.

Sheela,Ramu,Roop,and Mrs Seth all stood up together and had tears in their eyes. Ramu recognized his Sunday, Monday, Tuesday, Wednesday, Thursday, Friday and Saturday.

Ramu held his mother's hand tightly and said, "Ma see they look so sad."

Sheela said, "My darlings…they must be missing us. God knows if they have given them something to eat or not. My poor fellows…. I want them back anyhow."

Roop was busy thinking of the idea of setting them free from the circus.

Roop sat down and said, "Ramu, we need not waste a minute now. First, let us see what have they taught them in a few hours."

First, they set the dogs free. The four dogs were well trained. Their trainer was the same tall man who had come to take the monkeys. Roop gave a weird look on seeing him.

She turned towards her Nani and Sheela and spoke softly, "He is the one…. I am sure he is the one."

Ramu asked her, "Who is he now?"

"There were two men who had come. One is the clown, and the other is this dog trainer," said Roop pointing towards the tall man.

The dogs were a complete source of entertainment. They danced to the music, played with the ball and jumped to eat their biscuits.

Children laughed and shouted with excitement on seeing them.

The announcement began again with the beating of the drums, "The most thrilling show is about to begin…. Have you heard such names of monkeys…? we have…. see now…Sunday…. Monday, Tuesday…. Wednesday…. Thursday…. Friday and Saturday… come on."

ORIENT
CIRCUS

Ramu and Sheela looked at each other with their mouths almost open.

He said, "Ma, how do they know their names."

Surprisingly, Mrs Seth looked at Sheela and said, "It seems to be so strange that they know their names."

A trainer entered in a black satin dress with a red cap.

"Ma see Santosh Uncle. How could he do all this? He was dad's best friend."

Sheela's face became red with anger. "So he is the one who helped these two kidnappers. Your dad trusted him, and he betrayed us.

The cage opened, and the monkeys were pulled out by Santosh one by one,

"Sunday…. Come on……come out……Monday you old and lazy ones …. Tuesday…. Wednesday…… Thursday……Friday….and this last one Saturday."

Chapter Nine

The monkey show began, and the children were enlivened by seeing seven monkeys with such names. The monkeys knew their characters so well.

Even the children started calling out, "Sunday…. Monday."

The monkeys were not at ease, so they kept looking all around. They were tied with heavy chains. They were not listening to their present master.

Suresh, their new trainer, took out a stick whirled it all around. He then started playing the pellet drum.

The four of them sat stiffly on their seats, waiting for the right moment.

He kept playing the pellet drum and called out, "Come on you Sunday and Monday…the old ones…. more experienced ones."

As the monkeys did not move from their place, he struck them with the stick.

Ramu and Sheela stood up from their seat and were about to move towards them when Mrs Seth stopped them.

Roop could not wait any longer. She said in an angry tone, "Nani let us go out and call the police. We cannot wait anymore. We have very little time."

She quickly stood up from her seat, "Okay, I will go with Ramu. In the meantime, you keep them engaged as it may take even longer. We may have to file a complaint."

They rushed out while Roop jumped inside the arena, and Sheela followed her.

Suresh was shocked to see his friend's wife. The circus guards and other people rushed towards Roop and Sheela.

Roop freed herself and ran towards the monkeys. Sheela and Roop started calling them by their names.

Roop was running around, breathing heavily but still calling out, "Sunday……Saturday…. don't worry…. we are here. The monkeys seemed to have recognised, and they started pulling their chains. They wanted to be with Sheela.

All the monkeys started chattering and screeching. Chaos and confusion started building up among the circus workers.

ORIENT
CIRCUS

Sheela, who was held by two guards too, started yelling, "Leave my monkeys …..you cheaters…thieves and Suresh you."

Roop kept running all around, and four people followed her. She had to keep them busy until Mrs Seth was back.

People thought it was some kind of game. They had a great laugh with children almost holding their stomachs.

Suresh was catching hold of all the monkeys by their chains. He kept ordering the monkeys, "Come on Tuesday and Wednesday, start dancing."

The monkeys had turned a deaf ear to him now.

Chapter Ten

Ramu and Mrs Seth found two policemen standing outside. They reported to them the entire incident.

One of the policemen with a protruding stomach said, "Did you file a complaint."

Ramu started crying, "No, sorry, Police uncle. Can we file it now?"

Mrs Seth requested, folding her hands, "Please hurry up…. look at Ramu…. poor innocent child."

He picked up the Police radio and said, "Have patience let me connect to the nearby Police Station."

He connected to the nearest Cantt Police Station and filed the complaint on their behalf. He called three more police officers standing outside and moved towards the entrance gate.

"Come, Madam, I will catch them by their neck. Running their circus with stolen animals. They will be punished."

There was pin-drop silence the moment the four policemen reached inside. They went straight to the monkeys.

Roop stood near the monkeys and started rubbing them. They looked happy and confused.

Ten people from the circus staff entered and tried to settle the entire happenings. They were shocked to see the police.

One of them dressed in a white coat and pants spoke in a dominant tone, "Yes, I am the manager. Why have you come up? We don't need the police force. What is the matter?"

The policeman said, pointing towards the monkeys, "These seven monkeys do not belong to your circus. You have stolen them."

He replied, "No, we have bought them."

"What? It is impossible as they are my monkeys," shouted Ramu.

Roop said, "Police uncle, I have seen the kidnappers. They are working in the circus. One is a clown, and the other is a trainer. Do arrest him before they escape."

The circus men looked at her surprisingly.

One of them said, "Oh really…call them."

ORIENT
CIRCU

All the clowns and trainers were called. The police officers were happy to see such a brave girl. She recognized them, and the police soon captured them.

Roop cleverly got all the monkeys together and loosened their chains. She offered them peanuts and bananas.

Sheela told the police, "Sir, please catch hold of Suresh as he must have shown them the way. He keeps coming to my house."

The police officers handcuffed Suresh. He started crying, "I am sorry, Sheela and Ramu. I sold your monkeys for two lakhs."

All the people were dumbfounded on hearing the amount.

Roop said, "Police Uncle, Ramu is very poor, and he is unable even to provide food to these animals. Please think about him."

On hearing Roop, the policeman thought of a plan.

He said, "Now the punishment is that either you will have to return the money to Ramu or give him a job in your circus."

Mrs Seth and Roop smiled on hearing this idea. They looked at Ramu and Sheela. They eagerly waited for the reply.

Sheela nodded her head gently.

The circus manager agreed to keep the monkeys with Ramu and his mother. They wanted this new show to go on.

Sheela said, "Ramu, this opportunity will help us in making the rest of our life easier. Please don't refuse."

Ramu looked first at Roop then at Mrs Seth.

He said softly, "Thank You."

They thanked the police and returned home with the seven monkeys.

A bus came stopped in front of Ramu's house the next day. The Circus manager had come along with the two kidnappers.

Ramu and Sheela came out with their luggage. Roop and Mrs Seth had tears in their eyes.

Roop said, "All the best, Ramu. Take care of your weekdays and continue with your studies."

Sheela came and hugged her tightly, "I am speechless…. you helped us out, and we are no more having hungry sleepless days and nights. Thank you, Mrs Seth. Take care of my house. We will keep coming."

Saying this, she handed the keys to Mrs Seth, and Ramu touched her feet.

They sat in the bus with the monkeys and waved goodbye.

Ramu shouted, "Goodbye Roop…..Goodbye Aunty…See you soon."

9 789356 671720